Bayberry Island

HENRY COLE

Bayberry Island

An Adventure About Friendship and the Journey Home

KATHERINE TEGEN BOOKS
An Imprint of HarperCollins Publishers

Katherine Tegen Books is an imprint
of HarperCollins Publishers.

ISBN 978-0-06-224551-9

Typography by Carla Weise
17 18 19 20 21   CG/LSCH   10 9 8 7 6 5 4 3 2 1
❖
First Edition

Contents

Bayberry Island

chapter 1
The *Captive*

Twig's furry paws were sore. Gripping the spokes of the *Captive*'s wheel for three days had turned his pads from pink and tender to tough and calloused.

His body was sore, too. The *Captive* had sailed through a maze of floating debris and an endless series of rapids, with Twig guiding her every mile. His arms twitched from exhaustion.

His legs were tired from balancing. Tiny scratches marked where his toes had gripped the wooden planks of the deck.

But Twig's confidence had grown, as well as his muscles.

He gazed ahead, alert, looking for floating hazards and telltale signs of ripples and rapids. Things that had seemed so foreign just a few days ago were now a part of him: the patterns of water currents, the shadows of the clouds, even the smell of the river was like a friend.

A shout came from the crow's nest above him. "Looks like a log up ahead, on the right!" Basil was at his usual perch.

"Yep, I see it!" Twig shouted back. "Thanks, Basil!"

"When do we get to wherever we're going?" the weasel called down. "Can't we pull ashore somewhere?"

Lily stepped beside Twig, grinning. "How about it, Twig?" she said. "Want me to relieve you at the wheel? Then you can take the crow's nest and Basil can rest. He's still looking a little woozy."

Twig and Lily were quite adept at life on the water, but Basil had had a tougher time finding his sea legs. The swaying of the mast as the wind rippled the sails didn't help.

Lily glanced toward the rear of the ship. "And Char could use some attention," she added.

Char lay draped and drooping across the deck of the ship, eyes half-lidded, and his scaly skin grayish and dull.

Twig looked at the dragon. "I thought the fresh air was doing him good, but now I'm not so sure. He looked better three days ago."

"I know," Lily replied. "I keep hoping we'll see some signs that we're close . . . close to finding Char's home."

Twig nodded, then shouted up to the crow's nest. "Come on down, Basil. We're switching off!"

Basil made his shaky way down the rope ladder from the crow's nest. He looked green.

"Can't you make the *Captive* stand still?" he moaned. "I feel like I've been swinging on a vine for three days."

Lily handed Basil a rose hip. "Here. Chew on this. It may help settle your stomach."

Basil, looking queasy, munched halfheartedly on the rose hip, and Twig sat beside Char. He stroked the dragon's smooth scales and scratched under his chin. Char seemed to barely notice. "Lily, he's not doing so great. I hope we're going in the right direction . . . for Char's sake!"

Lily nodded solemnly. "Let's get him home." She took her position at the ship's wheel.

Twig thought, for the hundredth time, of home. He missed the delicious meals prepared by his mother, Olive, and the cozy comfort of his cottony bed.

He missed his conversations with Beau and wondered what Beau would think of him now. Would he approve of sailing off to an unknown destination, just to deliver a baby dragon to his home? "Beau would be proud of me . . . I know he would," Twig said to himself.

Even though their days had been busy, Twig knew that in between learning to sail and exploring the river, Lily was missing home, too. A pang of guilt passed through his thoughts. If it weren't for him, and his discovery of Char, they'd both be safe at home, not on the *Captive*, in the middle of the river.

He scampered up to the crow's nest and tipped his nose into the breeze. The scent of the river made his spine tingle with pleasure. Water gushing over stones and swirling between rocks was like music to him. Dozens of bright-blue damselflies came to rest on the railing of the *Captive*, and jittery water striders skittered out of the way as the ship plowed past.

The view from atop the mast was exhilarating. The river had widened, opening up their view. He'd never seen such an expanse of sky before, with only a few distant trees obstructing the panorama. The evening before they had sat on the deck of the ship and watched, enraptured: the setting sun turned a scattering of clouds into a gold-and-orange necklace above the dark-purple horizon.

And the vegetation was different than it had been upriver. The tangle of vines along the cliffs and banks

had given way to prickly shrubs and tall, rippling grasses.

Twig scanned the horizon ahead. "Keep her steady!" he shouted to Lily below.

"You got it!" Lily called back. "Twig, am I imagining things, or does the current seem slower? We seem to be slowing down!"

Twig watched the bow of the ship as it sliced through the water. A breeze was pushing at the sails, but the water was like glass. "You're right, Lily. There is definitely less current."

Far off in the distance he saw a hazy line stretching across the river. As the wind nudged them closer and closer, he began to make out the jagged shapes of sticks and branches jutting out of the water.

"Something . . . straight ahead!" he squeaked. "Not sure what it is, but"—he glanced left and right—"I don't see a way around it. It's like a wall!"

Basil seemed to stir from his woozy lethargy. He scampered to the bow. "A wall? Are we going to crash?"

"At the rate we're going, we will," Twig shouted back. "Sails down! We have to slow down! Everybody, grab a rope quickly!"

In a rush the three friends pulled at the series of ropes, working together and rolling the sails up to the masts, then lashing them down. As they worked, the *Captive* slowed some, but still drifted toward the dangerous line of branches.

"Oh my gosh!" Lily squeaked. Her ears cocked forward in alarm. "We're heading right into it!"

"Keep working at the sails, Lily. We're slowing down. . . . I think we may stop in time!"

Little by little, the ship slowed, and the last sail was tied to its mast. Finally the *Captive* sat still in the water.

The evening breeze had died. Twig raced to the bow of the ship, gripping the railing. "It's a wall!" he murmured as Lily and Basil joined him. They stared at the massive tangle of limbs. "A wall of trees!"

chapter 2

Rose Hips and River Water

The sun was just dipping below the horizon; darkness would soon be upon them. There was no reason to try to explore the wall or find any way around it. Basil set the anchor for the night.

Nervous about the barricade looming over them, and chilled by the nighttime air, they tossed uneasily on the deck of the ship, sleeping fitfully when they could. It was still dark when they heard the first distant morning birdsong. They stretched, shivering and stiff.

Lily sent a bucket over the railing and hauled some

water up, as Twig examined their cache of food. "Looks like the last of it," he said. "We're going to have to find some more food soon. We have a few rose hips left, and some acorns. Not much."

"Rose hips and river water, rose hips and river water," Lily said. "Wouldn't a nice, steaming cup of sassafras tea be good right about now?" She smiled wistfully. "And a walnut muffin?"

Basil frowned at her. Being seasick had made him thin, and grouchy. "Please. Don't mention food."

From the deck, Twig and Lily nibbled acorns and examined the giant wall. In the dim morning light they could see that the wall stretched from one side of the river to the other, an enormous distance. It was constructed of thousands of branches and limbs and sticks. Mud was chinked in between, and in many places grasses and weeds and small trees had taken root in the mud. The massive structure towered above them.

Just then the morning sun poured onto the river, illuminating the landscape. "It's a beaver dam!" Lily exclaimed. "Just like Professor Fern told us about. I've never seen one, but that's got to be what it is!"

Twig grinned. "Of course!"

"Well, what good does that do us, knowing that it's a beaver dam?" Basil said. "We're still blocked. We can't go forward and we can't back up. We're stuck."

Twig looked thoughtfully at the dam. "Maybe if we get on top of it, we can see if there's a way around it."

"How are you going to do that, Twig?" Lily asked.

"I'm going to jump. From the crow's nest I can make it to that overhanging branch. See?" He pointed to a sturdy-looking limb that jutted out closest to the *Captive*.

With that, Twig scurried up the rope ladder to the crow's nest. The jutting branch was tantalizingly close, but dangerously distant.

"Are you sure you can do this?" Basil called up.

"We'll find out!" Twig called back.

"Gruk!" croaked Char with concern.

Just as Twig was crouched and ready to leap, another voice called out.

"Hello!"

They looked up to see the cheerful face of a beaver beaming at them from the top of the dam. "Hello there!" it said again.

"Hello!" shouted Lily. "Good morning!"

The beaver was dark and slick as it moved agilely over the mountain of branches and made its way to the

edge of the river. "Good morning to you!" The beaver stared at the *Captive*. "My, you've found an interesting way of travel! I've never seen such a thing!"

"We're trying to get downriver," Twig explained. "But your dam has blocked our way. Can you help us?"

The beaver looked at the ship. "Hmm. Yep. Think so." With that, it scrambled across the dam, and then returned shortly with a length of grapevine.

"Here! Tie this somewhere, and I'll pull you to a good spot. You'll see!"

Lily lashed the vine to the railing on the bow. "Ready!"

With the other end of the vine in its mouth, the beaver began to tug. Slowly the boat began to move through the water. The beaver ducked under and climbed over and around the myriad of limbs, pulling the *Captive* along the edge of the dam.

Soon they heard the gushing sound of rushing water. "A break in the dam!" the beaver called out. "Lucky for you, but on our checklist to repair it today."

"Huh?" Twig shouted.

"Don't worry! You'll make it!"

The current began to carry them through the opening in the dam.

"But careful of the waterfall!" the beaver warned. "The current may be a little strong!"

"Now he tells us!" Basil moaned, grabbing onto the railing.

A torrent of water poured through the break in the beaver dam, and the *Captive* wobbled and swayed.

"Hold on!" Twig yelled.

Lily gave a yelp. "Whoa!"

The ship pitched and dipped as it was carried through the dam, down, down, down a series of waterfalls and rapids. Several times it nearly capsized, careening side to side.

One sail was snagged on a sharp branch, turning the boat around and causing it to spin in circles.

"Make it stop!" Basil squeaked. "Please make it stop!"

Suddenly, with a splash, the ship plunged through the dam and into the calm water on the other side, the current pushing them along into open water again.

"G'bye! Safe journey!" They turned to see the beaver calling to them from on top of the dam.

"Thank you!" Lily answered back.

The morning sun warmed their backs as they hoisted sails and caught a stiff breeze from the south. Twig's whiskers twitched in the wind. He stood at the wheel and pointed the *Captive* downriver. It felt good to be moving again.

Lily sat with Char and held his head. The dragon blinked and looked out across the water. He seemed to sense something. "Char knows we're trying to help him," she said.

Twig nodded. "I hope we're on the right track."

Basil was at the railing, looking miserable. "What's

that?" He pointed to some floating vegetation. "It looks funny."

They were sailing through small patches of green aquatic plants that swirled and danced as the ship passed.

"They may be edible," Lily remarked. With that, she darted down to the ship's hold and rummaged through their collection of vines and ropes, then carried them up onto the deck. It wasn't long before she had fashioned a small net and was dragging it through the water.

"Here! Let's see what we've got," she said, hauling the net up with its tangle of green weeds. She munched on a leaf. "Not bad!"

Twig took a nibble. "Agreed! It's pretty good!"

Basil looked gray. "No thanks. I can't handle green and squishy."

But Char looked up from his spot on the deck and sniffed.

"Here, buddy," Twig said, offering the dragon some of the slick, wet sea grass. "Hey! He likes it!" Char gobbled up the offering, then sniffed for more. "This is great! We found something Char likes!"

Basil looked even worse as he watched Char munching the greens. "I can't take it!" And he raced to the back of the boat.

The crew was exhausted, after a sleepless night before and the strenuous day. With the warm sun on their tired bodies, they collapsed on the deck and slept.

Twig woke up to the sound of a rasping snore and looked over to find Char snuggled up beside him, sound asleep.

Night had fallen. He looked up to see a half-moon, and millions of stars, brilliant and sharp, like silent frozen sparks. He quietly wiggled away from Char and stood at the railing on the bow.

They had slept, and sailed, through the afternoon and halfway through the night. A breeze swept over the *Captive*, salty and fresh. The water was choppy, with swells that gently caressed the boat.

Twig looked across the water. He could not see any trees or shrubs or grasses in the moonlight; the horizon was a straight line.

They had reached the ocean!

chapter 3

Hot Air

The night turned to day, then to night again, then another day. At first, the reality of water stretching from horizon to horizon was a little unnerving. The only sounds were the wind in the sails and the splash of the waves against the bow. But Twig saw how Char would lift his snout into the air and breathe deeply; the dragon seemed to be blissfully enjoying the new smells.

The excitement of finding themselves in the vast ocean didn't last. It wasn't long before they wished they could see even a glimpse of a bush or a tree, and the unending ocean was monotonous . . . and a little scary. And their food supplies were running out.

After a week on the open water they awoke to an eerie stillness. The breeze that usually picked up as the sun rose never came. The sails on the ship hung limp.

"What do we do now?" asked Basil. "We're just sitting here." Although he was relieved not to have the usual stomach-churning lurch of the water, it was a little disconcerting to be motionless in the middle of the sea.

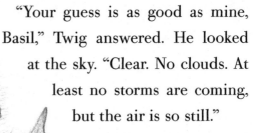

"Your guess is as good as mine, Basil," Twig answered. He looked at the sky. "Clear. No clouds. At least no storms are coming, but the air is so still."

Char snorted and pointed his snout to the air. He was looking a bit better. The seaweed diet seemed to help.

Lily giggled. "We should get Char to flap around. His little wings could stir up a breeze."

"Hey!" Basil said. "Why not use Char?"

"Seriously, Basil?" Twig replied. "Those little wings couldn't stir up enough breeze to sail a ship!"

"You're not thinking. What if Char made a little breeze using something else? Maybe some hot air? He could blow us around."

"You may have something there, Basil," Lily said. "He could snort at the sails and conjure up enough wind to take us somewhere."

Twig pulled at his whiskers and then shrugged. "Why not? Let's give it a try. Char? You feel up to an experiment?"

Char gave Twig a puzzled look and then followed him toward the stern. "Okay, buddy," Twig said encouragingly. "Give it what you've got." He pointed Char's head in the direction of the sails and stroked

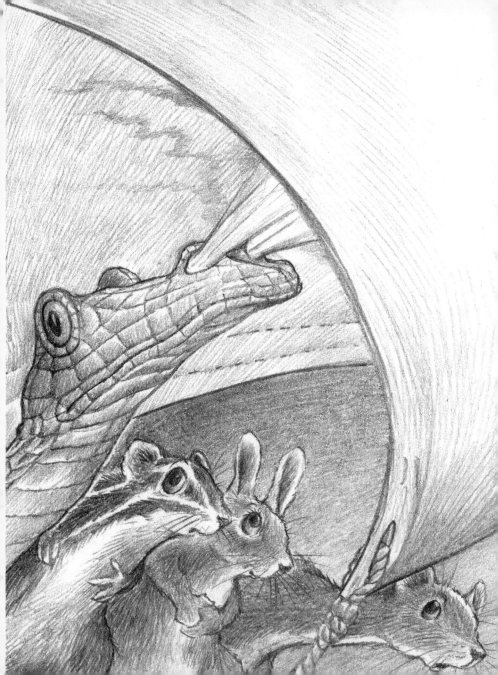

the dragon's chin gently. Char gave a snort, then a sort of burp, and he jerked his neck back. A moment later a puff of smoke, and then a blast of fire, shot from Char's nostrils.

The accompanying hot air pushed at the lower sail. The canvas flapped gently. The *Captive* moved forward a bit.

"Attaboy, Char!" Basil shouted. "See? I knew it would work. Try it again, Twig!"

"Well, it's working," Lily commented. "But I can tell it took a lot out of Char."

Char's velvety wings drooped, and smoke curled from his nostrils. He looked a bit exhausted.

"He's just getting started. Let's do that again, Char," Basil insisted. "Twig, stroke his neck again and let him give the sails another blast."

Again Twig gave Char a series of caresses, and again Char's forceful blasts pushed at the sails. Over and over they cajoled Char into blowing the sails, and the ship moved in spurts across the water.

But the effect was not worth the effort: Char was soon weakened and drained. The *Captive* had gone only a short distance. The crew abandoned the idea.

But as they sputtered through the sea, Lily noticed that their dancing ship attracted dozens of tiny silver fish. The fingerlings darted this way and that around the stern of the ship, like fleeting bits of foil in the green water. She got an idea.

She went below, into the hold of the ship, and then hauled up all sorts of vines and old twine, heaping them onto the deck and plopping herself in the

middle of the pile.

Then her paws began moving rapidly in sync.

Basil was perplexed. "What in the world are you doing now?" he asked. "Here we are stuck in the middle of who knows where, and you're weaving? Are you crazy?"

"Just wait. You'll see."

Twig was just as puzzled but kept quiet. Before long he saw that Lily, using her knowledge of knots and weaving, had begun to fabricate a long net.

She worked diligently. By the end of the afternoon, she was finished.

"Here, hold this end," she said to Basil, handing him one end of a long coil of vine. "Twig, you take this end." With Basil and Twig positioned on either side of the stern, Lily tossed the mass of net off the end of the ship.

The net floated just below the surface and opened up like a flower blossom. They watched as one by one, the tiny silver fish came to the net to explore. Curious, several swam inside the opened end.

"See?" Lily whispered. "They're swimming inside."

"Then we pull the net onto the deck?" Twig whispered back.

"Uh-huh, exactly."

They surveyed the scene as the small fish continued to swim in and out of the net, getting more and more at ease with the strange object which was looking like a mass of seaweed floating in the water.

"When do we pull it up?" Basil asked.

"Just a little more time," Lily breathed. "When I say *now*."

A dozen of the fish were in the net. Lily nudged her friends. "Now!"

With much splashing and a frenzy of commotion, they yanked on the ends of the net and pulled it up onto the deck. Most of the silvery fish had slipped away, but several of them thrashed and flipped and sputtered on the planks, eyes wide and gills pulsing.

"You did it!" Twig cried.

Lily grinned, blushing.

Basil was still not in the mood for eating. "What do we do with a bunch of fish?" he asked.

"They're not for us, silly," Lily responded. "They're for Char!" She picked up one of the slippery, wiggling fish and offered it to the baby dragon. Char greedily gobbled it down and looked for more.

"Hey! Excellent!" Twig shouted. "Lily, you're a genius. Char looks excited. He's feeling better already!"

Lily proudly offered Char another fish, then

another. It was good to see him sitting up, his wings fluttering and eyes a little brighter.

"Hey! What's that?" asked Basil, pointing up at the sails.

Small puffs of wind were massaging the canvas.

Twig cheered. "Hurrah! The wind is picking up. Finally!"

"Now maybe we can get somewhere," said Basil. "This life on the ocean is for the birds. Or the fish, anyway."

The breeze picked up.

They raced around, tightening lines and making sure the sails were ready for the wind. Twig took his place at the wheel.

"I'll take crow's-nest duty," Lily said as she darted up the ropes.

The breeze became a bit more brisk, and the *Captive* began racing across the waves. Lily found herself gripping the railing of the crow's nest tightly. "Steady as she goes!" she shouted down.

She looked off to the horizon, and the fur on her
neck stood up.

"Twig! Basil!" she cried out. "We may be in for it!"

They all looked off to the west. The sky behind them was black and ominous. Dark clouds were roiling and banking. The sun disappeared. A thick blanket of storms was heading right toward the *Captive*.

chapter 4

Just Hang On!

The canvas sails billowed and flapped as the wind whipped into a gale. Twig gripped the wheel tightly, pointing the *Captive* with the wind. The ship plunged up and down with the waves, and water began to splash over the deck.

Char fluttered his wings, his claws scraping and sliding across the slippery planks. Twig glanced back at the dragon. "Basil!" he cried. "Hold on to Char!"

He was nauseous and green from the tossing boat, but Basil struggled to reach Char, and then flung his paws around the dragon's neck, holding on tightly. "It's okay, Char!" he moaned. "This won't last long . . . I hope!"

Up in the crow's nest, Lily squeaked in terror as the mast swayed dangerously low from side to side, then back and forth. Twig yelled above the roar of the wind, "Lily, come down!"

Lily tried to make her way down the ladder. Her tiny paws slipped on the ropes as the wind tried to grab her and toss her out to sea.

Then the rain came. A few enormous drops fell at first, and then a pounding torrent. With the blowing sea and the thundering rain, water seemed to fill the air.

Lily shrieked as she lost her grip and slid down the slick ropes, landing with a thump.

Sore and limping, she clung to the railing and moved up beside Twig at the wheel.

Twig was struggling. His arms were no match for the roaring wind. The wheel spun rapidly one way, then the other. It was impossible to control it.

"What do we do?" Lily shouted, futilely trying to wipe the rain from her eyes.

"Just hang on!" He looked back to see Char scraping along the wet, slippery deck, making his way forward. The dragon tucked his wet snout under Twig's arm, shivering. "It'll be all right, Char!" Twig comforted him. But the rain slashed at his face and he winced and choked.

Basil joined them, and they all huddled together, clinging to one another against the raging maelstrom.

A blue-white flash of lightning was immediately followed by a terrifying crash of thunder. A sudden gust of wind and rain tipped the *Captive* dangerously to starboard. Instead of righting itself, the ship leaned more and more.

"What's happening?" Basil screamed.

"Char!" Twig grabbed on to the dragon. "Everybody! Hold on!"

"We're tipping over!" Lily shrieked as another gust of wind hit the sails. In seconds the boat lay sideways in the water, tossing in the waves.

They all thrashed and splashed, trying to stay afloat, and then climbed onto the swamped tangle of masts and sails and ropes.

"Char! Char!" Twig called out as he looked for the baby dragon in the waves.

Char had found the floating crow's nest, which had broken off as the ship tipped over. The dragon was bobbing up and down, wings fluttering. Twig made his way over, arms and legs flailing in the water. "Good boy!" he shouted, clinging to the wooden basket.

Lily and Basil struggled over. They gasped and gulped in between waves.

The storm raged on. Waves and wind blew the tiny crow's nest farther from the wrecked *Captive*. In between flashes of lightning, Twig saw the ship turn over and its hull point to the sky.

The storm began to lessen as quickly as it had begun. The pounding rain became a steady shower. The raging wind turned into a series of gusts, then a gentle breeze.

Off to the east, the storm continued, with distant flashes of lightning and far-off rumbles of thunder.

Twig squinted in the near darkness. His eyes searched for the ship. "Look!" he shouted.

They all turned their heads into the breeze.

The bow of the *Captive* pointed into the air. Her majestic mast and sails were under water.

"Oh!" Lily murmured sadly. No one else spoke as they watched the beautiful *Captive* sink into the sea.

THEY CLUNG TO THE OVERTURNED CROW'S NEST THROUGH the night, shivering. The moon rose but provided no warmth.

The three friends were silent, paddling to stay alive.

Char was still. The others hugged him close in an effort to keep his body temperature up. He was dangerously cold.

Twig wondered if he would ever see home again.

Finally it brightened a bit to the east as morning came.

Twig was chilled to the bone and despondent when he heard a voice.

"Hello!" someone called out. Surprised, Twig looked across the water to see an enormous turtle staring at him. The turtle was golden and brown, with friendly eyes peering from her glistening scaly face.

Lily and Basil brightened. "H-hello!" Lily called, her teeth chattering. "H-help!"

The friendly face disappeared into the water. A moment later, the turtle surfaced right below them, and

they found themselves sitting on the turtle's back. "How's that?" the turtle called over her shoulder. "Better?"

"Th-thank y-you!" Twig said, almost giddy with relief. His arms and legs were exhausted, limp from overexertion. He sat up on his elbows. "I . . . we . . . can't thank you enough!" he said.

"Now what are you good folks doing out in the middle of the ocean?" the sea turtle asked. "You don't see many like you out this way." She looked at Char questioningly.

"Our sh-sh-ship. It sank," Basil replied, shivering.

"Oh! Out on a ship, huh? Yep, big storm last night." The turtle nodded at Char, who was gray and still. "Your friend all right?"

Twig covered Char's cold body with his own. "He's barely with us. We need to get him somewhere warm."

"Sun's coming up. Gonna be a nice warm day," the turtle said. "I'll get you to a good place. Hang on!"

With that, the turtle began paddling. Strong flippers pushed them across the water with amazing speed.

"Doing all right up there?" she asked.

"Just fine!" Twig replied, happy to be in the turtle's care.

Before long they heard the sound of surf up ahead, and soon the turtle was dragging her heavy body up onto the gritty shore.

They hopped off the turtle's back, and then carefully helped the barely alive Char onto the warm sand. Twig looked at the smiling turtle. "I don't know how to thank you," he said earnestly. "You saved our lives."

"Yes!" Lily agreed. "How do you say thank you to someone as good as you?" She smiled and brushed some sand from the turtle's face.

The turtle grinned. "You are most welcome. Glad to be of assistance. Hate to say it, but you're on your own now. Be careful. Best of luck to you!"

With that, she slowly turned her heavy body back into the waves. After a few strokes from her strong front flippers, she disappeared.

They saw her head bob to the surface some distance out, and she waved. Then she was gone.

chapter 5

Sand Dunes

After days on the water, land felt strange but glorious. The warm sand beneath their toes was solid and steady.

Char stretched his body out in the sun, looking a little more alert. The radiant sun on his scales was rejuvenating.

Twig looked cautiously at the sky. Instinctively, he knew the danger of being on an exposed beach. He examined the dunes away from the shoreline. "Let's get out of here," he said. "This way."

They staggered and scrambled along the wet beach and then the dry sand until they got to the base of a series of enormous dunes. There didn't seem to be anywhere to go but up.

"Well, maybe from the top of these mountains we can see exactly where we are." Twig sighed.

"Char, do you think you can make it?" Lily asked. She stroked his face with concern.

"He can do it," Twig remarked.

"Sometimes I think Char is invincible! C'mon, Char."

They struggled up the steep, sandy slopes. The sand was loose, and the breeze from the ocean blew it in their faces. Sometimes they lost their footing and slid back down in a cascade of furry feet and sand.

The going was treacherous, but after much effort they mounted the crest of the tallest dune. They stood on the crest and gazed around.

Off to the east was the ocean, vast and undulating.

"We were out *there*?" Basil gasped, as they finally saw the enormity of what had been their watery world.

Twig thought sadly of the *Captive*, lying at the dark bottom of the sea.

They turned to face west. Before them lay a forest of scrubby pines and shrubs. Suddenly the sand beneath their feet collapsed and they tumbled and slid down the other side of the long, steep dune. Down, down, down they fell, tumbling head over heels until they landed in a heap. An avalanche of white sand continued to fall, nearly covering them up.

Coughing and spitting sand, Twig dug his way out. "Lily! Basil! Are you all right?" He pulled at the thrashing arms and legs of his friends and spotted Char's wiggling tail, giving it a yank. Soon they were all shaking sand off and brushing it from their eyes.

"Everybody okay?" Lily asked, examining the crew. "Char?"

Char looked a little bewildered but unscathed.

Twig looked up the side of the dune. "Looks like we found the fast way to the bottom!" He laughed.

They were all tired from a night in the water. The warm sand felt good.

"Let's rest here for a while," he said. "Regain our strength. Something tells me we're going to need it."

Not far away was a small clump of vegetation. Twig pointed to it. "It isn't much, but it's some protection. Let's use that as a place to catch some sleep."

After they nestled beneath the prickly leaves, the extent of their exhaustion hit them. Lily was bone weary. Twig was drained. And Basil was the worst off.

He hadn't eaten in days and was drained of all energy. "I can barely keep my eyes open." He yawned. In a moment he was asleep, his furry face in the sand.

Twig covered Char's tail with the warm sand and made little mounds of it on his back. Char closed his eyes. In minutes they were all asleep.

Twig awoke. He wondered where he was. It was dark, but he didn't recognize the fuzzy, prickly leaf that tickled his ear.

There was sand beneath him.

Then he remembered; the storm, the sinking, the sand.

Night had fallen. He was finally warm again after sleeping for hours on the sunbaked dune. He glanced over at his friends. Basil was asleep, although fitfully, and his tail and paws jerked in a dream. Lily stirred a bit. Char was still tucked under his blanket of sand, snoring.

Twig ducked beneath the prickly leaves and cautiously poked his head out into the nighttime air. He heard, far off, the rhythmic crashing of waves on the shoreline. He sat in the sand and looked up. The stars were shining, brilliant against the black of night.

The leaves rustled, and Lily emerged from their hiding place.

They sat and watched the sky. A shooting star zipped across.

"I see some of the same stars from home," Lily said at last. There was a wistful note to her voice. "I wonder if my parents are looking up and seeing the exact same stars."

"You wish you were there now? Home?" Twig asked quietly.

"Uh-huh."

"Me too."

"But this has been quite an adventure."

Twig swallowed a nervous lump in his throat. "You sorry you came along?"

"Nope."

"I'm really glad you did."

Lily giggled. "I can see you trying to sail the *Captive* without me. You'd never make it!"

Twig smiled, and then thought of the beautiful ship,

lost forever. "We made a great crew," he murmured.

"Yep. She was a great ship."

"Question is, how're we getting back, once we get Char to where he needs to be?"

"And that's a good question, Twig," Lily replied.

They both curled up in the sand. Another shooting star split the nighttime sky.

chapter 6
Lily and the Lasso

The morning air was filled with the shrill sounds of calling birds. These weren't the melodious songs of woodland birds that Twig was used to, but raucous cries and harsh squawks. It made it even clearer that they were in a foreign, unknown environment.

Under the canopy of the little shrub, Twig shivered. Were the birds overhead friend or foe?

Basil poked his head out from under the leafy tent. "What is all the racket?" he groaned.

"Careful, Basil," Twig said. "Who knows what may

swoop down? We don't know what lives here." Basil ducked back into the safety of the leaves.

"Of course," Twig continued, "we'll have to find out. We need to find food, as well as find out where we are, and where we go next."

He cautiously scampered out of the shrub and glanced around. There were birds soaring and gliding in the sea breeze overhead. Twig made a loud chirping sound to attract their attention, and then readied himself to dodge back into the vegetation.

He looked up. Several of the birds cast him an offhand glance, but none of them looked the least bit interested. Perhaps he wasn't considered food in this dune environment.

"I think it's okay to explore," he said.

They warily trooped out, stretching in the morning sun and shaking off sand. In a moment they realized that they were at the bottom of a deep pit, bounded by mountains of sand. The walls of the pit were steep and on all sides.

"We're surrounded," Basil said. "Sand everywhere."

They all tried climbing up the loose slopes, but each time slid back down in an avalanche of sand.

"We need to get out," replied Lily. "But not sure how."

They debated different ways of getting out. Basil suggested climbing on one another's shoulders.

"That's fine for the first one out," said Twig. "But what about the last one?"

"Well, the first one out can be a . . . a scout," Basil retorted. "And report back to the rest of us."

"And who wants to be the scout?" No one spoke up.

"Okay. Next idea."

Char was doing his own exploring and started digging in the sand some distance off. "Look!" Lily pointed. "Char's feeling better. He's finding his own way out by digging a tunnel!"

They watched as Char got deeper and deeper into the sand, until only his rear half was showing. He snorted as the sand flew behind him, his wings shaking and fluttering. Suddenly the hillside of sand collapsed around him, and the dragon was left buried, with only his thrashing, wiggling tail exposed. In a moment his head popped out of the loose sand, and he snorted a puff of smoke.

Laughing, Lily raced over and began pulling on Char's tail, while Basil and Twig dug out the sand around him.

"You're no help," Twig said. "We can't spend all day rescuing you!"

Lily surveyed the plant life that dotted the bottom and slopes of the pit. She thought of the crow's nest of the *Captive*. "Should be easy to fashion a rope," she said. "If I can find the right materials. There's not much to work with, but I can do it."

She got to work. Using twigs and various vines she gleaned from around the pit, she made a rope long enough to reach the top of the sloping walls. One end she tied into a loop.

"If we give each other a boost, we can maybe lasso that sturdy-looking shrub up there." She pointed to the north edge of the pit. "Then we just pull ourselves out, paw over paw."

"What about Char?" Twig asked.

Lily thought for a moment. "We boost him up first. He's the first one out."

"Okay. Let's try it."

Basil crouched down, and Twig climbed on his back. Then Lily, with the lasso at the ready, scrambled

up onto Twig's shoulders. With many attempts, she was able to hook the end of the rope around a strong-enough branch of the shrub high above.

"Great!" she squeaked. "Now let's get Char out of here first."

"Come on, Char," Twig coaxed. "Climb onto my back."

Char clambered up Basil's furry back and then Twig's legs. With wings fluttering, he made it onto Lily's back.

"Hey! Hurry up!" Basil cried out. "I'm getting crushed down here!"

With a flurry of wing beats and a giant push by Lily, Char scrambled over the edge of the dune pit and onto the rim.

"Hurrah for that!" Lily called. "Now my turn."

Paw over paw she pulled herself up.

Basil came next. He was weak from days of no nutrition. It was a struggle, but at last he lay gasping at the top of the dune.

Finally it was Twig's turn. With the combined efforts of Lily and Basil pulling on the rope, he was at the rim of the pit in no time.

Panting heavily, they surveyed the scene around them. They could finally get a good look at their surroundings for the first time. All the sandy dunes were part of an island, surrounded by sea. The birds that swooped and soared above their heads were seabirds, gulls and terns and sandpipers, calling to one another, agitated by the intruders below.

The birds were strange, with unusual colors and patterns and calls. He wondered what other creatures were on the island.

And were they friend, or foe?

chapter 7
Strange Berries and Bugs

"I think we'd better look for cover, someplace where we aren't exposed to . . . well, to anything," Twig said. "Someplace safe."

"Safe? From what?" Basil asked, looking furtively around.

"Safe from predators, of course," said Lily. "As far as we know, we're moving targets. Let's get off these exposed dunes."

Twig scanned the area and pointed off in the distance. "See the green areas over there? Looks like lots of plants are growing there. And I'm betting there may be the possibility of fresh water, too."

Basil was still looking nervously at the sky. "Yeah . . . let's get out of here. I didn't survive a sinking ship just to end up in the claws of some hawk!"

They left their high perch on top of the dune and traveled along its ridge to an area of undergrowth and

shrubby vegetation. There were small trees and bushes, and small herbs and flowering plants.

Few of the plants looked familiar. Some had odd-shaped leaves, or thick, prickly skin. None of the trees grew tall, but were bent and curved and stunted from the ocean wind. But Twig was relieved to find that they provided dense cover. He kept his eye open for good spots to spend the night.

Many of the plants were covered in berries. Lily discovered some blue berries growing in clusters on a low shrub. "I'm tempted to eat these," she said. "They look a little like the blueberries we're used to, but . . ." She hesitated. "What do you think?"

Twig and Basil examined the fruit. Twig

took a small bite out of a berry. "Tastes the same as blueberries back home!" He nibbled some more. "Tart, but delicious!" And with that, they ate berry after berry. It was the first real food Basil had eaten in days, and he devoured them. He was beginning to look like himself again.

Twig poked his whiskers into a low shrub. It was thick with rose blossoms and small red fruits.

"And over here!" he shouted. "I know rose hips when I see them." He chewed through the tough skin. "Yep! Just like the kind my mom used to make into pies."

Lily noticed a little plant that grew low to the ground in dense patches. It was brilliant green and unlike anything she had seen before. She sniffed it, and then nibbled one end. It was salty and delicious. "Tastes good!" she said. "And sort of crunchy!"

They soon found several different kinds of nutty-tasting seeds, as well as low-hanging plums and a variety of berries. Everyone was excited to find foods that were edible; now they knew they wouldn't starve.

Even better, they noticed Char pouncing on several bugs he saw darting about. The dragon was looking better than he had in weeks.

The warm sun, the fresh ocean air, a good night's sleep, and now the discovery of delicious food brightened everyone's spirits. Even Basil laughed a little as they watched Char chase a yellow butterfly.

They trekked lower and deeper into the dense under-brush. The air didn't stir. The ridges of dunes muffled the sound of the pounding surf, and after that they heard only the chirping of birds and the drone of insects.

The bird sounds grew louder, and the vegetation grew thicker and greener. Soon they discovered a quiet pool of water, clean and fresh after the heavy rainstorm the night before. They drank greedily.

"Ah . . . tastes so good." Twig sighed. He looked around. "Maybe this is a good place to spend the night, maybe set up a temporary home until we figure out where we go next."

Lily agreed. "Food, water, shelter. Everything we need."

"Yeah, for us and who else?" Basil interjected. "If it's a good place for us to be, it's a good place for anything else. Ever think about that? Who knows what's out there, ready to pounce on us?"

"Any other suggestions?" Twig asked.

"Well . . ." Basil hesitated. "At least let's have shifts. Two of us sleep while the other keeps guard. Then we change places. At least until we know what it's like around here."

"Good plan, Basil," replied Lily. "Let's find a place to spend the night. We'll find some dry grasses and make sleeping places, gather some berries and things to have them on hand. Then we'll figure out who's on what guard shift. Okay?"

"Okay!" Twig agreed. The three of them set off to gather things to make camp. It felt good to have something constructive to do. Twig was very happy that his two friends were with him. It would have been tough by himself.

The only thing that darkened Twig's mood was

the fact that they didn't seem to be any closer to finding Char's home. There were no signs of dragons . . . although Twig wasn't sure what signs to look for! Tracks? Or burned places? He looked at Char for indications that he somehow recognized where he was. But nothing happened.

If this *wasn't* Char's home, then they were shipwrecked.

chapter 8

Surprise at the Campsite

The campsite became home right away. They chose
an enclosed, protected nook that was tucked under
a low-hanging evergreen, near a freshwater lagoon. Old
pine needles formed a kind of screen on three sides.
Made with dried grasses and sweet-scented leaves of
bayberry and juniper, the beds were soft and comfort-
able. Lily found an oyster shell and dragged it over to
the site, and they filled it with the seeds, berries, and
other fruits they gathered. Twig was delighted to dis-
cover sassafras trees growing nearby.

Basil was back to normal. Fresh food, and being back on dry land, had restored his health. Lily kept busy, picking berries and keeping Char company, but Twig noticed she was looking pensive and distracted at times. "I think we should have a meeting," he declared. "And decide what we're doing next."

Lily looked relieved. "Good idea, Twig." She pulled some large leaves into a circle for their powwow.

"Okay," Twig began. "First of all, I think we . . ." He stopped. They heard a rustling in the underbrush behind them.

Basil gulped. "Did you hear that?"

Twig glanced around. "Yeah."

"Me too," Lily whispered. "What was it?"

The air was silent, except for a slight breeze whooshing

through the bayberry branches.

Twig listened for a moment, then continued. "Like I was saying, I think we should start to . . ."

They heard the rustling again, closer this time.

Lily pointed to a dark area of ferns and fallen pine needles. "There!"

Several sets of eyes were peering at them from the shadows.

"Run!" Twig shouted. "Char! Follow us!" The trio took off toward the lagoon, Char fluttering his wings alongside them. They slogged through the shallows, hopping from sand bar to sand bar, and along fallen branches, and sliding across patches of slippery rotting leaves.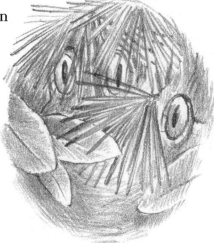

They heard splashing behind them as their pursuers chased them through the dark water. "Don't look back!"

Lily squeaked. "Just *go!*"

They reached the opposite side of the shallow lagoon. A wild tangle of greenbrier vines faced them. Thick and nearly impenetrable, the vines were covered with sharp thorns. The thorns snagged and tore at them as they dug their way through the leafy tangle.

Suddenly Char snorted in pain as one of his velvety wings was cut by a series of thorns. He stopped, gingerly fluttering the wounded wing.

"Char!" Lily shouted, frozen in her tracks.

Twig stopped and turned. Char was definitely wounded. But the ripping and tearing of vegetation behind them got louder.

"Come on, Char!" he begged.

Basil, panicked, pushed aside the stabbing briars and scrambled up a stunted pine.

The three friends froze in terror as the loud crashing got closer.

Suddenly the crashing stopped. Twig closed his eyes, preparing for the worst. He heard panting and snorting. He opened one eye.

There, looking at them, were several baby dragons!

chapter 9

Toot Sweet!

Wow!" Lily exclaimed.

Basil remained clinging to his perch in the pine. "What a relief . . . I think!"

Twig stood motionless, awed by the sight of three other baby dragons. They varied a little in color, but otherwise were identical to his beloved Char.

Char gave a loud snort. His eyes turned golden yellow-orange as he galloped through the vines to the other dragons. They all fluttered wings in rapid beats, while dodging and dipping their long necks in greeting.

One of the dragons stretched its neck and gave a tooting squawk. Suddenly the rest of the little group stretched out their necks. In a cacophony of toots, they trumpeted greetings, louder and louder, a frenzy of emotion and excitement.

Char trembled a bit and stopped fluttering his wings. He hesitated, and then stretched out his neck, too. After a giant intake of air he gave a loud, squeaking squawk, like the sound of a rusty trumpet. The other dragons responded with another flurry of elated squawking.

Twig laughed, delighted. "I think we've found Char's home!"

Lily clapped her paws, her whiskers twitching with pleasure and relief. "I think so, too! These must be Char's brothers and sisters!"

The dragons gathered around Twig and Lily and began sniffing and tasting them with snorts and licks. "Stop that!" Lily giggled, convulsing on the ground as the dragons continued to shower them with slurping pink tongues.

Basil watched the scene from his perch on the pine branch. "Well, now what do we do?" he asked, finally dropping down from his hiding place. "We've found Char's home. We've gotten him back to his family. How about *us*? What do *we* do? Where do we go now?"

"I hope Char's parents are this friendly," warned Basil. They had all been pondering the kind of reaction they would receive from Char's family. "I hope they know that it hasn't been easy getting Char back here. I mean, throwing up over the side of a ship for three days wasn't my idea of fun."

Twig giggled. "Maybe Char will tell them, in his own language. He talks now!"

He looked nervously around. "And where are Mom and Dad?"

Basil nodded. "Exactly. Maybe the the parents would eat us?"

"Don't be silly, Basil," Lily said. "Do you really think Char would let that happen?"

"Who said Char was in charge?" Basil replied. "He's only had you and Twig around. Who knows what his natural instincts are really like? I think it might be a *good* thing that there are no parents. Look, we've brought Char home. Now let's figure out a plan to get *us* home!"

Twig was silent but had to agree. Maybe it was time to head home. But how?

Char squawked loudly. One of the baby dragons had stretched his neck and blown smoke. It rippled and

coiled into the air like magic. Another of the dragons blew several puffs in the shape of rings, which expanded wider and wider as they rose into the air.

Char seemed to study the other dragons as they puffed and snorted, and began mimicking them. He was learning to be a dragon. His nostrils flared as he puffed several smoky rings.

Two of the dragons snorted and began fluttering their wings in rapid beats, faster and faster. The wings became a blur and suddenly created a humming, vibrating hum. The other dragon joined in, and then Char started his own wing-song.

Whirrrrrr!

Twig twitched his whiskers, enraptured. "Listen to that! It must mean they're excited, or happy!"

"It's amazing!" Lily agreed.

The wing vibrations continued. "Maybe they're trying to call to their parents," Basil suggested nervously.

The three friends looked around, wary of what might be tromping through the underbrush at any minute.

Basil continued, "I still say they may have lured us here, just to pounce on us."

"Basil, you're crazy," Twig replied. He looked at the wildly humming dragon wings. "They're happy, they're excited, they're being baby dragons, that's all."

Lily nodded in agreement. "But keep a sharp lookout, just in case," she said.

The wing vibrations stopped and the cluster of baby dragons began to sniff and explore, squawking to one another. It was as though they were becoming better acquainted with Char.

Twig watched them for a moment. Then a worrying possibility crossed his mind. He turned to Lily and Basil. "Hey. I wonder . . . what if we're *not* in the right place?"

"What do you mean?" Basil asked.

"I mean, what if this *isn't* Char's home? What if . . . ?"

"What if *what*, Twig?"

Twig gulped. "What if these baby dragons are just like Char? Orphans?"

Basil considered this. "You're thinking that maybe we just landed on an island with other baby dragons? That it's just a coincidence?"

"Well, yes. Maybe."

Lily's whiskers drooped. "Then maybe they're here in the same way that Char ended up near the Hill."

Twig nodded. "You know that big storm the other night? Well, what if there were other storms, just like that one? Or even worse? What if there was a storm big enough to blast eggs out of a dragon's nest and wash them away?"

"There's no telling how many eggs could have ended up all over the place," Lily added.

"That means that Char's parents could be any-where," said Basil. "They could be on this island, or . . . any island. They may not even be alive at all!"

They all looked at the baby dragons, watching them snorting and puffing and fluttering. No one said it, but they were each thinking the same thought: Had they just inherited a whole new baby dragon family?

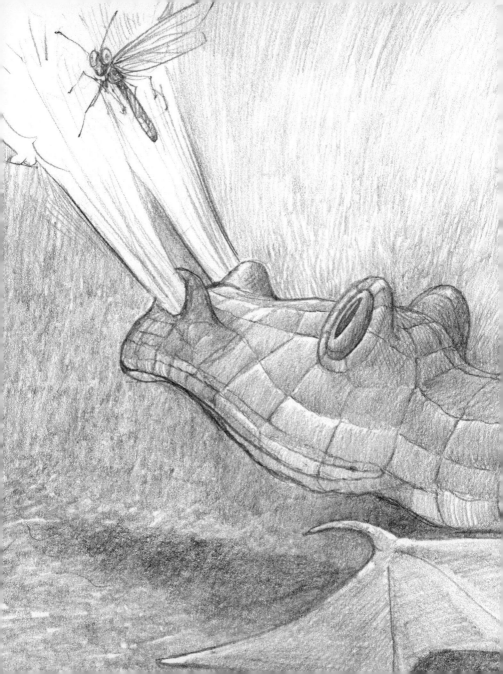

chapter 10

Show-offs

The dragons spent the day comparing their flame-throwing abilities. With the food and fresh air, Char had regained all his strength. His fire-snorting nostrils were in fine form.

With much aplomb, he showed off in front of his newfound siblings. He zapped a katydid on a distant tree limb. He made a target out of a knothole, hitting it perfectly each time. He brought down countless flying insects with his spewing flames.

The other dragons were suitably impressed but

had their own fire-breathing prowess to display.

One dragon burned through a pine branch. Another fluttered briefly over a puddle and shot flames at the water; the water sizzled and boiled.

Lily shaped the white sand into sloping piles and watched as the dragons shot fire at them. They soon turned them into glistening cones of hot glass, experimenting with other shapes and making interesting patterns with the molten glass.

Lily delighted in making the dragons silly little hats and bows, which she wove from leaves and grasses and decorated with flowers and red berries. She enjoyed just sitting and watching the drag-ons for hours.

She saw one of them snap at a bee. "I think I'm going to name you . . .

Bee!" she laughed. "And you"—she glanced at another of the babies rolling in the warm sand—"you're Roller!"

She glanced around for the third dragon, finally spotting him resting in the shade of some ferns. "And you're Shadow!"

Lily smiled as she watched the baby dragons head off into the undergrowth, and then return after a bit, holding some sort of prize in their mouths. Many of these prizes were unknown to Lily: strange, wiggling centipedes and hard-shelled crustaceans and horned insects. Lily knew they were supposed to be gifts, and special treats, but they looked foreign and unappetizing.

In a sudden inspiration, Lily thought of getting Char to roast the treats. She placed them on a shell, and Char or one of the other dragons would quick-fire the crickets or katydids or one of the other island creatures. The flames roasted them, making them much more edible.

Lily dragged a deep clamshell into the clearing

and filled it with a variety of ripe berries and water. She coaxed Char to flame the shell and boil the water repeatedly; after stirring and mashing the berries, she made a sort of jam. Char heated up another shell filled with grass seeds, toasting them. Lily sprinkled the toasted seeds over the jam. "Not as good as the berry pies and tarts back home, but not bad!" she said, sampling her experiment.

And, after roasting and dipped into the berry jam, the mysterious and odd centipedes or mole crabs made a tasty snack.

But Basil was less interested in the dragon hijinks. "Maybe it's best to be far away from the baby dragons, just in case the parents finally show up," he said bluntly, and then slipped off into the brambles. Later, he returned, pulling some pine needles over his body as camouflage, and napped in the shade most of the day.

Twig decided to explore the island a bit. He climbed to the top of several dunes, cautiously watching for predators. From each viewpoint he saw only an expanse of shrubby trees, tangled vines, and undergrowth, and more dunes in every direction. The far-off roar of the surf sifted through the salty air.

He discovered broad stretches of sandy soil, flat and sunbaked. Thousands of seabirds dotted the terrain and filled the sky above, chattering and calling. Twig saw fluffy baby birds, squatting on the sand among broken bits of shell, and nearly hidden with their camouflage coloration.

Within the shade of the shrubby pines and bayberry bushes, the air was hot and still, but filled with the incessant sound of chirping and clicking insects. The heat of the day didn't seem to deter them.

He heard a loud, raucous croaking sound and looked up through the branches of a scrubby pine. A monstrously large bird, with long legs dangling down and a long, sharp beak, was flapping slowly overhead. Twig cowered, motionless, until it flew past.

He scampered back to the clearing. Lily was playing with Char and the other dragons. Her cooking experiments were scattered around the site, and the dragons were adorned with various woven hats and bows. He laughed.

Then he had a sudden pang of sadness that he'd have to give up Char someday and they'd have to part. Char had become like family to him. He wished somehow they could stay together.

As the shadows of the afternoon got longer and longer and evening fell, the trio gathered the dragon babies around them protectively.

Using Char's flame, Twig started a little campfire of dry pinecones and leaves. They sat around, eating from their cache of food, staring at the flames, lost in thought.

Home seemed far away. None of them had any idea of how to return there.

Basil fluffed up his bed of dried grasses and lay there, thinking of home and how to get back.

The baby dragons piled one upon the other, with their heads and necks tucked under one another's wings. Soon they started to snore, and puffs of smoke drifted up into the pine boughs above. Every now and then one of them would snort and their wings would quiver, and then they would settle down again.

Lily tiptoed over and slid in among them, her arm around Char's neck, and closed her eyes.

Twig looked at Char and smiled. It had been a long time since he'd seen the dragon look so healthy or contented. That alone was worth the arduous trip down the river, the treacherous storm and shipwreck, and the unknown of their present situation.

Crickets called to one another, scattered about the tangle of bushes and vines. Twig recognized the distant song of a mockingbird.

He looked up to see a few stars, in between the branches of the bayberry bushes. The same stars were watching over the Hill. He suddenly had a terrible yearning to be back home, in his own bed.

chapter 11

An Unexpected Visitor

After a few days it became apparent that Char's parents were not going to appear. Char and the rest of his clan seemed perfectly capable of surviving on their own.

Twig called a meeting. "What do you think about figuring out a way to explore around the island? Maybe there are similar, neighboring islands nearby?"

"And maybe Char's parents live there," Lily suggested.

"Exactly."

"Who says we want to find Char's parents anymore?" Basil asked. "He seems okay to me. Maybe there aren't any parents. But I can tell you one thing: he is doing perfectly fine . . . and we should head home."

"Well, maybe it *is* time," Twig said solemnly. "We've done our duty, Char is safe and with his brothers and sisters. Now I guess it's time for us to head home." He paused, looking anxious. "Any ideas of how we go about that?"

"You brought us here. Didn't you think about how we'd get out of this mess?" Basil blurted out.

"Basil, nobody knew the *Captive* was going to sink," Lily interjected. "Be reasonable, for once."

Twig said, "Well, a boat got us here; a boat will have to get us back."

Lily frowned. "There are certainly no ships in bottles around here. We were so lucky before, finding the *Captive*. That will never happen again!"

Twig nodded. "No, this time we'll have to make

something. I suggest finding a big enough log or limb, something that floats."

Basil chuckled. "You're both loony. Make a boat out of some sort of stick?"

"We can do it, I know we can," Twig said. "Let's go down to the beach and start there. Look for something that might work. At least get ideas."

"You two go ahead," Basil said. "Find something, let me know. Sounds like a waste of time to me."

"Why don't you at least try to find some good vines for weaving into ropes, Basil?" Lily suggested.

"Yeah . . . okay," he replied, sauntering into the underbrush.

Twig and Lily headed down to the shoreline, scouting for an easier passage through the dunes. They scanned the area for anything that could be used for boatbuilding. They poked around at a few possibilities, but the wooden pieces that they found were crooked, or rotting, or waterlogged, or too big or too small.

Lily squinted into the distance and then pointed down the beach. "See that, Twig? Way off? That log might be perfect!"

The log was fairly straight. It had been washed ashore at some point and lay just out of reach of high tide.

"I'm thinking," Twig said. "With Char's flame, and the other dragons, too, we could burn the log, a little bit at a time, and chip it out. Dig out the inside, making a perfect boat."

"Great idea, Twig," said Lily. "And this branch? Maybe it could hold a sail?"

Twig's whiskers twitched. "We're as good as home! Let's go get Char and the rest and get to work."

They returned later to the beach, this time with the little troupe of dragons in tow. After scouting around, they found some sharp-edged shells that could be used

as scoops and digging tools.

With the baby dragons working together they burned and charred the dead wood of the log bit by bit, inch by inch, and then picked and tore at the burned wood as they went.

"Hey . . . where do you think Basil could be?" Lily wondered aloud, as they toiled at the smoldering wood. "He should be here helping."

"Who knows. He'll probably show up right as we finish this. What do you think we could use as a sail, Lily?" Twig asked.

"I saw some large leaves before," she replied. "I can't think of anything else on the island that would work."

"Me either. Maybe we could sew leaves together into a sail. Or maybe we could paddle."

"Wow . . . that'd be tough going."

"I know, but . . ." Twig looked out across the water at something that had caught his eye. "Look, Lily. Out there beyond the crashing waves."

A dark object was bobbing up and down over the swells, too far out to distinguish, but close enough to know it wasn't floating driftwood, or a turtle.

"Oh my gosh, Twig," Lily gushed. "You don't suppose it's . . . another boat?"

"That'd solve everything! A boat comes to *us*!" They gazed off over the water, ears cocked forward and whiskers twitching.

"Either we have a new boat, or we ask if we can hitch a ride!"

The object floated nearer, rising on top of a swell,

but then disappearing as it rode
down into a trough, appearing
and disappearing over and over
as it dipped up and down.

Twig climbed up the
crooked branch of the fallen
log to see better.

"It's a boat, all right,"
he called down. "I can
see there's someone in it.
Apparently the boat has a
captain!"

"Does he look friendly?" Lily hollered up. Her ears
rippled in the ocean breeze.

Twig had read about pirates in several of his old pic-
ture books, and he squinted to see better. "Can't tell yet!"

Still the boat washed closer to the beach, riding
the frothy surf up onto the beach. Twig scampered
down the log and joined Lily on the sand. They ran to
the water's edge.

The figure in the boat was hunched over. But there was something familiar about his shape and the color of his fur. And as he turned and sat up, Twig could see the distinct shape of a pointy snout.

Twig stared, then rubbed his eyes and blinked. He couldn't believe what he was seeing.

"Professor Burdock!"

"Surprised?" Burdock said as he stepped from his boat, a reconfigured wooden guitar. He dragged it by a tuning peg across the wet sand.

"H-hello, Professor!" Lily shouted above the surf. She stared in disbelief.

"Lily," he replied, coldly returning her stare. He then turned his gaze to Twig. "And dear Twig. A pleasure, at long last." His bared his teeth in a sarcastic smile. "Didn't expect to see me riding over the waves to your little desert island, did you?"

"N-no, Professor," Twig stuttered. "How did y . . . ?" He stopped, suddenly aware of the smell of smoke. He turned his head toward the dunes to see a trail of

curling smoke that rose above the beach grasses.

There was a shout from up on top of the dunes as Basil appeared, waving and grinning.

"Uncle Burdock! Hello! Am I glad to see you!" He scurried down the sandy slope of the dune and ran across the beach.

"You saw my signal smoke? You knew it was me?"

"Yes, Basil!" Burdock answered. "Saw your clever smoke and knew exactly who was signaling me. Very smart boy!"

"I used embers from our campfire and dried seaweed to start the fire, then added damp things to make the smoke." He gestured at Twig, laughing. "He had no idea! They never saw the smoke!"

Twig was amazed, but angry. He had always thought Basil had been napping, or lazing off, when actually he had been starting signal fires! He gritted his teeth, his whiskers twitching.

"Like I said, very clever boy," Burdock said. "I saw your smoke miles away." He stretched his long neck and shook his tail. "It's been a long trip!"

"You mean, you *followed* us here?" Twig asked, eyes wide. "You knew where we were this whole time?"

"I have been following you, yes. Nearly paddled my arms off, I'll admit that. When I got to the open sea, I wasn't sure which direction you had gone. Leave it to my ingenious nephew to direct me."

Basil grinned. "Thank you, Uncle Burdock."

Twig looked at Basil incredulously. "You mean you were in on this the whole time?"

Basil snorted. "Of course."

Burdock chuckled, too. "All part of our plan."

"How did you get past the giant beaver dam?" Lily asked, still incredulous.

"I threatened those idiotic beavers. What ninnies. Several of them carried my boat over the dam. No problem."

"And the storm? Did you get into a storm on the ocean?" asked Twig.

"Oh, yes. That irritating storm popped up. But

see?" Burdock pointed to a well-constructed lid that covered up the sound hole of the guitar. "Designed it myself. And I huddled inside until the storm was over. Warm and snug . . . safe and dry . . . easy as that! Rode out the storm, no problem."

Twig and Lily were astonished. They had wondered how everyone was at home, and here was someone *from* home, but their least favorite someone!

And Basil had known all along that they were being followed!

Twig's whiskers twitched. There was just one unanswered question that he needed to ask.

Why was Burdock here?

chapter 12

Trapped

Back at the campsite, Burdock's eyes widened when he saw the small tribe of baby dragons. "My, my!" He chuckled. "This is a very pleasant surprise! More little furnaces for me! It will be more of a challenge to get them back home, but what a boon for business when I do."

"What do you mean?" Twig asked. "You're taking them back to the Hill?"

"Of course. Certainly you don't think I would come all this way for nothing."

"But why?"

Lily piped up. "You want to hurt Char, I know it! You can't take him with you. We nearly died getting him back here! This is where he belongs, with other dragons like him." She looked at Twig with questioning eyes. Char was not with the other dragons. Twig shrugged and decided to keep quiet. But his eyes said, *I don't know where he is!*

Burdock slunk around the campsite and poked the dried-grass beds with a stick. "Humph," he continued. "All these dragons belong where I say they belong. And I say they should be at the Burrow of Smelting, working for a living. I can make quite a profit using all these little fire-breathing creatures . . . to make all sorts of goods. They'll be a good asset for the community, not to mention my pocketbook."

"What do other Guild members say about this?" Twig asked.

"Other Guild members are clueless. I'll be running things."

He glared at Twig. "And you . . . *you* were the one to use the dragon for your own benefit!"

"But I didn't know that Char would become so sick. When I saw what it was doing to him, I stopped. I had to get Char home!"

"When you stole that creature out of the Guild prison that night, I couldn't believe my bad luck. I had made plans! And you put a glitch in those plans. But that's why I followed you to this forsaken place, so that I can keep things just the way I had planned them!"

Twig was furious. The day had become a nightmare. Not only was Burdock, his only enemy, here on his island, he was kidnapping Char and returning him to the Hill!

119

"You're not taking Char, Burdock!" Twig replied angrily. "Or any of the baby dragons! Not if I can help it!"

"Well, it seems there isn't anything you can do to stop that from happening." Burdock smiled, turning to Basil. "And where is our little fire-breather?"

"He's right where we want him, Uncle," Basil replied.

"What? Where's Char?" Twig shouted.

"Basil, why don't you take us to him?" Burdock smiled. He looked very suspicious.

"Certainly, Uncle. He's . . . this way," Basil coaxed, and pointed through the bracken and weeds up a sandy slope. The baby dragons stood rooted in place, their faces quizzical.

Lily and Twig scooted between the vegetation, anxious to find Char. They suddenly came to a little clearing and stopped. Dense foliage and brambles surrounded them.

"Now!" they heard Basil shout, and in seconds they were tangled in a net, struggling and thrashing. A moment later Basil and Burdock had tied their paws.

They were prisoners.

"Well done, my boy!" Burdock exclaimed. "I never cease to be amazed at your achievements!"

"I just kept all of Lily's weavings and made them into this. They were such jerks. Thought I was sleeping all the time. Doesn't take much to set a trap!"

"And now?"

"Now we take them to a special place. They know all about it. We were trapped there ourselves on our first day. They'll be there long enough for us to take the dragons and go."

Basil and Burdock dragged and prodded Twig and Lily to the giant sand pit beyond the dunes. They pushed them down the slope, with their paws still tied behind them, and the two plummeted down the sandy sides, head over tail. They landed in a heap at the bottom of the pit.

"Oh dear," Burdock exclaimed. "You're right, Basil. That is quite a deep pit. And it looks quite difficult to escape from it."

"We had a tough time of it," Basil replied. "It took all of us, piled on each other's shoulders, to get out. They won't have that."

Twig pointed to the little shrub where Lily had thrown her lasso. "The rope is gone!" he said grimly.

Burdock turned to his nephew. "You have our special friend in a safe place?"

"Yep! I tied him with a leash. He's all set to go."

"All right. We gather supplies, and the rest of the dragons, and then we take off. I figure we can take our time; these two will be in this pit for quite some time. In fact, who knows if they'll ever climb out?"

"Good-bye!" Basil called, laughing. "Don't let the sea hawks get you!"

Twig and Lily struggled, rolling in the sand and trying to squirm out of their bindings. It was no use; they were tied tightly with strong honeysuckle and greenbrier vines. The greenbrier cut into their paws and wrists, and gagged their mouths.

Lily's eyes were full of panic. Even though Twig couldn't understand her muffled squeaks, he knew exactly what she was thinking: *What do we do?*

Twig tried to speak through his gag, too, but it was useless. *Poor Char!* he thought. *They'll make a prisoner out of him. We need to think of some way to get out of here! And if we don't think of something soon, we may be stuck on this island forever!*

chapter 13

A Giant Shadow

Lying on his side, Twig wiggled over to Lily and began to chew at her bindings. It took a while, but eventually her paws were free and she could untie Twig and remove their gags.

"They were idiots to think I couldn't chew my way out of some silly honeysuckle vines," Twig said.

Lily spit out some bits of vine. "Twig, what if they run off with Char and the rest? How can we stop them?"

"Haven't figured that out yet. It was tough enough getting out of this pit the first time."

They looked up at the steep incline. Loose sand slid down the slopes.

Lily paced and fretted. "I can't stand the thought of Burdock and Basil with the dragons. They don't know how to care for them!"

"I know. We have got to get out of this pit. Come on, let's try again."

Repeatedly they attempted to scale the slope, falling back to the bottom in a pile of white sand.

"If only I hadn't already used the last bits of vine," Lily moaned.

"We'd still need a boost of some sort. It's no use, Lily. We're trapped. And no food or water."

Just then a shadow fell over the pit. It grew and grew until it covered them.

They instinctively dove headfirst into a sandy pile. "Hide, Lily!" Twig squeaked. "Cover yourself up!" The two of them dug into the pile of loose sand and scrambled to conceal themselves.

"It think it's a sea hawk, or some other huge bird,"

Lily shakily whispered through the sand. "It's something big . . . the shadow it cast was enormous."

"Let's hope it decides to fly away. We're trapped. Can't escape. Don't move!"

With a *BOOM!* the giant creature swooped down, shaking the ground and crumbling one side of the pit. Part of the rim of the pit collapsed as the sand cascaded down.

Twig and Lily burst out of their sandy hiding place. They looked around frantically, then saw the only possible out: in a flash they scrambled up the newly created incline.

Sand was flying from beneath their feet as they reached the top. But the shadow was still hovering over the pit.

Twig was nearly crippled with panic. He looked up. Whatever was creating the shadow was backlit against the bright sun. It was huge. It wasn't flapping or soaring. That was when Twig saw that it wasn't a bird at all.

It was a giant dragon. Towering, colossal, mountainous.

Twig and Lily gasped in unison. "W-what now?" Twig sputtered. Lily turned to race around the pit, and for a second glanced back down into the pit. Then she realized something. "Look. The pit!" she exclaimed. "Now I see! The pit is a . . . a giant *footprint*!"

They stared in shock at the huge print. The three giant toes and the shape of the foot in the sand seemed very apparent now. They had been so close they hadn't seen it. Now it was obvious: they were in the shadow of a very large beast.

They turned slowly to look up at the adult dragon.

Its large yellow eyes, flecked with gold, as high as a tree, stared back at them. Several hornlike nibs, purple and shiny, formed a crown on top of its head. Two turquoise wings, so much like Char's, but a much bigger version, undulated and fanned the air in broad swooping flaps. Bits of sand blew as the tips of the wings traced across the ground.

The dragon's scales were creamy white in front, and soft green down the back. Each green scale was decorated with a tiny gold dot, except for the scales down its spine, which were ridged and bumpy. The bumpy scales ended in a long tail that flicked and coiled and twisted through the air.

Twig and Lily were transfixed. Any attempt at running away seemed futile, so they crouched there in the shadow, paralyzed. Twig tried to speak, but could only stammer. "I-it's—it's—it's—"

"It's *beautiful!*" Lily whispered.

chapter 14

Guitar to the Rescue

Twig and Lily grasped each other as the giant beast lowered its huge head. It peered at them, first with one eye, and then the other.

"H-hello!" Twig ventured.

A sudden puff of smoke furled out of its nostrils, making Lily jump. "W-we are your friends!" she said nervously.

Twig found his courage. "Yes! We have been taking care of one of your babies!"

Lily ventured a smile, and waved. "He's been a good baby dragon!"

The dragon gave a huge snort, and more puffs of smoke jetted out.

"Uh, you may be really hungry," Twig continued bravely. "But we think maybe your babies are in danger!" He gestured with his paws for the giant dragon to follow. His tailed flicked with urgency.

"Yes! This way!" Lily exclaimed. She pointed and started to head down the slope into the underbrush. The dragon stood still, its tail waving and flicking.

Lily hesitated. "Do you think it understands?"

"I hope so. One way to find out. Let's go!"

With that, Twig and Lily darted off in the direction of Burdock and the dragon babies. They looked back over their shoulders to see the large dragon bounding after them.

They scrambled quickly through the

dense tangle of vines and underbrush, leaping over
fallen branches and prickly greenbrier, racing like
they'd never raced before.

The dragon had no problem keeping up, but followed them as if it knew where they
were leading. The sand around
them trembled as it bounded
along. Twig could feel the heat
on the fur of his tail, emanating
from the giant dragon's nostrils.

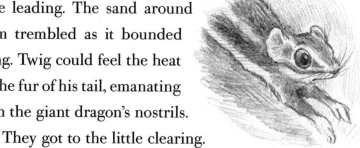

They got to the little clearing.
The baby dragons were nowhere to
be seen. Twig noticed signs of a struggle, and
several burned places. "Look. See that? I bet Burdock
upset the dragons. They probably tried to shoot flames
at him."

"I hope he got burned in the process!" Lily replied.
She looked up at the giant dragon. "It's okay. We'll find
them!"

"Let's try the beach," Twig suggested urgently.

"They may already be trying to leave the island."

They headed across the now worn pathway to the dunes. Beyond, they could hear the roar of the surf. At the top of the last dune, they could look down onto the sandy beach.

"There they are!" Twig pointed. Near the edge of the surf were Burdock and Basil. Char and the little troupe of baby dragons were being loaded into the guitar ship. Their snouts had been tied shut, and their tiny wings pinned tightly to their sides with strong vines.

The giant dragon lifted its head and let loose a loud, piercing bellow, then raced across the sand, Twig and Lily close behind.

Burdock looked up in horror to see the giant dragon, angry and still trumpeting its fury, galloping across the beach. He shoved the last of the dragon babies into the hold of the guitar boat, and then he and Basil began to frantically push the boat out to sea.

"Hurry, Basil!" he shrieked. "That must be one of the parents. We need to get out of here fast!"

"I don't think we can make it, Uncle Burdock!" Basil shouted back.

Burdock's eyes were wide with fear. The huge dragon was nearly upon them, with wings spread menacingly and streams of smoke trailing from its nostrils.

"There's nowhere to run now," Burdock shouted back. "Our only way out is across the ocean. Keep pushing this thing into the water! Push!"

But the huge dragon wasn't going to let them get away. It towered over them and began shooting streams of fire. Burdock and Basil abandoned the guitar boat, and then took off down the beach, streaking across the sand in terror.

With a few flaps and leaps, the dragon blocked them, and the two weasels skidded to a stop. The dragon bellowed again, and its tailed flicked and bobbed.

At the same time, Twig and Lily raced to the guitar boat. Char and the other little dragons were huddled inside. Twig yanked at Char, pulling him out onto the sand, and began to nibble and chew through the vine bindings.

Once free, Char began to squawk and flap. He saw the giant dragon and, with excited squeaks, scampered down the beach toward it.

The mother dragon turned away from Basil and Burdock and saw Char for the first time . . . with Twig racing behind. To the dragon, it looked like Twig was threatening her baby. Enraged, she turned her attention to Twig.

Hissing and bellowing with fury, she raised her head and neck high, preparing to shoot a blast of fire at the little chipmunk. She spread her wings. Twig, frozen with fear, could only prepare for the worst.

Suddenly little Char scurried in front of Twig, facing his mother. His wings fluttered rapidly and he trumpeted a series of little toots and squawks.

"Gruk!"

he croaked, again and again. "Gruk! Gruk!"

The mother dragon roared with excitement, sniffing and nuzzling Char and vibrating her giant wings. Char returned the affection, racing and skittering around the enormous feet of the mother dragon, flapping his wings and tooting.

Twig, relieved, looked over to see Lily at the guitar boat, smiling broadly at the reunion. "We did it, Twig!" she shouted across the sand.

But Burdock slithered up behind her and pushed her aside. "Out of my way!" he hissed. He quickly looked down into the guitar. The other baby dragons were sitting wide-eyed and bound. With the mother dragon distracted by Char, the two weasels pushed and pulled at the guitar boat, getting it closer and closer to the surf. A few moments later they had it out into the water and were hastily paddling it out to sea.

"They're taking the babies!" Lily shouted. "They're getting away!"

The mother dragon turned from Char and looked at the little boat bobbing over the swells. Steamy puffs of smoke snorted out of her flared nostrils.

This was not a happy mommy dragon.

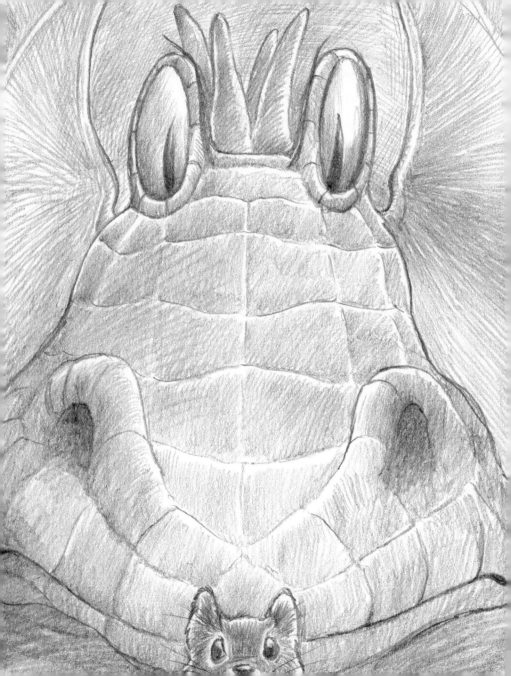

chapter 15

Home at Last

Incensed, the mother dragon sloshed through the surf. Her wings postured and spread threateningly. She towered over the little guitar boat.

Burdock lifted his paddle and swung it at the dragon. "Paddle harder, Basil!" he screamed. Basil tried to maneuver the boat in another direction, away from the menacing mother dragon.

But her huge head dropped in front of the boat. Burdock swung at her with his paddle, but the dragon took no notice. Instead, she began pushing the boat back toward the beach, nudging it over and over.

The bottom of the boat scraped into the sand. In a panic Burdock and Basil crawled out onto the neck of the guitar, and watched as the mother dragon gently pulled her babies out one by one and dropped them safely on the beach.

Then she again turned her attention to the two weasels.

With one toss of her head she flipped the boat end over end back into the surf. Burdock and Basil spilled into the water and floundered in the frothy waves, thrashing and spitting.

The dragon coiled back and shot a giant blast of fire that scorched the guitar. It smoked and smoldered in flames, and then, with a black hissing sputter, it sank to the bottom of the sea.

The two weasels frantically struggled back to shore. They were fairly good swimmers, but the mother

dragon caught them in no time. With a flick she tossed them onto the shore, where they sat, sandy, salty, and breathless.

The mother dragon turned to Twig and Lily. The hair on Twig's spine stood up as he saw her approach them, wings extended. For a second he thought she would scorch them, too, but she lowered her head and nuzzled them, pulling Char and her other babies under her protective wing.

Char had found home, at last.

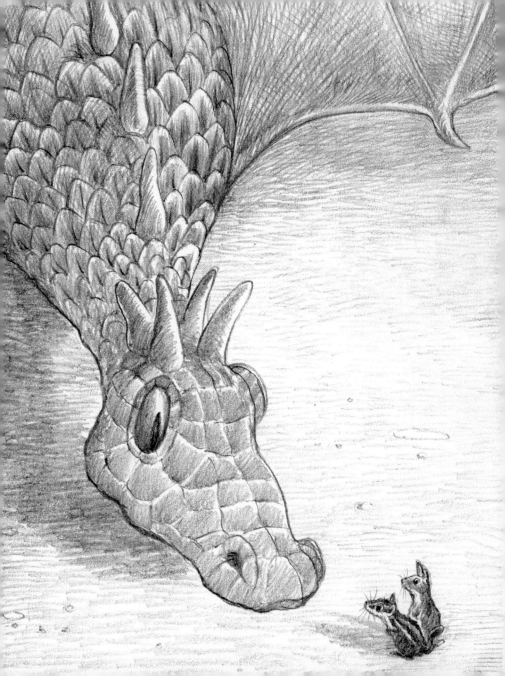

chapter 16

Good-bye, but Not Farewell

Twig sat on top of the giant dragon's back. The bumpy scales made great knobs to grip on to, and both he and Lily hung on tightly. It was exhilarating to be high atop the back of the enormous reptile. The beach was far below.

Char was back with his family, at last. Twig and Lily laughed as they watched him race with the other young dragons, flapping his tiny wings, running in circles and frolicking at the edge of the surf.

Twig figured a storm, or perhaps several storms, had raged through the area and separated Char's egg from the rest. The tough shell was resilient, and survived undamaged. Lily supposed that Char's mother took frequent trips to hunt, and that Char's siblings had been tucked away on a separate island for safety.

And now Twig and Lily, atop the giant dragon, were ready to head back to the Hill.

They looked down. Char sat on the beach below, gazing up at them, his tiny wings fluttering and beating with agitation. "I think he knows we're leaving," Twig said.

"Yes . . . he looks so tiny!" Lily sighed. "I'm going to miss him so much!"

Twig nodded. "He's taken us on quite an adventure.

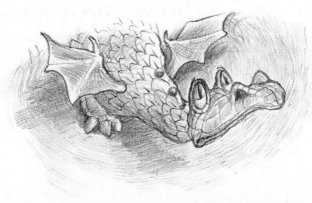

Think of all the things that
have happened . . . running
away . . . sailing a ship . . .
surviving a storm, and all
because I found an egg one
day on a muddy hillside." Twig
felt his heart fill with tender affection
for the little reptile. It was all worth it, just to see Char
with his family, happy at last.

Twig felt proud. He had returned the baby dragon
to his home.

He hadn't done it alone. He and Lily had been
on an adventure that guaranteed a lifelong friendship.
They had memories they could share forever, memories
that no one else would understand or appreciate.

Yes, there were big memory events, like hiding
Char from the Guild, and refurbishing and sailing
the *Captive*. But there were little memories, too: sharing a secret over a mug of sassafras tea, watching Char

chasing a butterfly, or studying the stars on an astonishingly clear night.

Maybe that's what friendship is, Twig thought. *Sharing things. The big, and the little.*

He glanced over his shoulder at Lily and smiled. She was waving good-bye to Char. He could see she was trying not to cry.

"Don't worry, Lily," Twig said. "He'll come see us. As soon as his wings are strong enough."

Lily laughed. "I hope so!"

Twig patted the giant scaly back of the mother dragon. It was time. "Let's go!"

The huge wings lifted and flapped

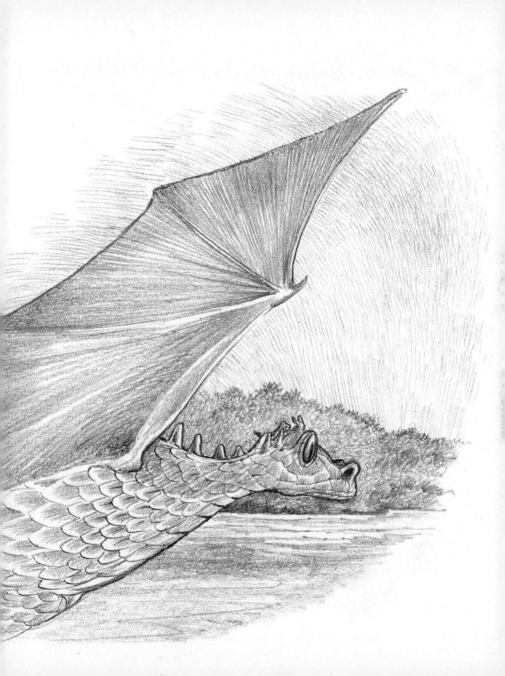

in broad, sweeping strokes. Twig and Lily pitched forward, then backward, their paws grasping the dragon's back. They rolled to one side as the mother dragon circled once over the beach.

They saw Char and the others racing under them, far below, until the ocean surf stopped them.

The dragon flew along the edge of the beach, following the curve of the island, and then swooped for a moment above a small cove. Burdock and Basil were sitting on the sand below, and looked up.

"We'll be back for you!" Twig called down. He saw Burdock's face darken with anger.

Lily laughed. "Well, *maybe* we'll be back!" she shouted.

The wind blew through Twig's whiskers. He looked ahead, over the dragon's head. The pang he felt in his chest was quickly turning into excitement. Heading home!

It wasn't long before they saw the hazy green line

of land far ahead of them, and then the broad expanse of a bay, and the silver rippling of a river. Twig tried to wave as they passed over the sturdy beaver dam. "Hello!" he called out.

The river narrowed, and the deep green of the Woods enveloped them. Twig began to smell the familiar scent of forest and soil.

They were home.

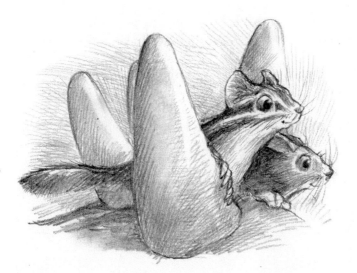

DON'T MISS THESE BOOKS BY
HENRY COLE

KATHERINE TEGEN BOOKS
An Imprint of HarperCollins *Publishers*

www.harpercollinschildrens.com